AT DADDY'S ON SATURDAYS

Linda Walvoord Girard
Illustrations by Judith Friedman

Albert Whitman & Company,
Morton Grove, Illinois

Also by Linda Walvoord Girard

Adoption Is for Always

Alex, the Kid with AIDS

Jeremy's First Haircut

My Body Is Private

We Adopted You, Benjamin Koo

Who Is a Stranger and What Should I Do?

You Were Born on Your Very First Birthday

Library of Congress Cataloging-in-Publication Data

Girard, Linda Walvoord.
  At daddy's on Saturdays.

  Summary: Although her parents' divorce causes her to feel anger, concern, and sadness, Katie discovers that she can keep a loving relationship with her father even though he lives apart from her.

  [1. Divorce—Fiction. 2. Fathers and daughters— Fiction] I. Friedman, Judith, 1945-   ill. II. Title.
PZ7.G43953At 1987   [E]   87-2126
ISBN 0-8075-0475-0 lib. bdg. ISBN 0-8075-0473-4 pbk.

The text of the book is printed in fourteen-point Fairfield.

Text © 1987 by Linda Walvoord Girard.
Illustrations © 1987 by Judith Friedman.
Published in 1987 by Albert Whitman & Company,
6340 Oakton Street, Morton Grove, Illinois 60053-2723.
Published simultaneously in Canada by General Publishing, Limited, Toronto.
Printed in the U.S.A. All rights reserved.
10 9 8 7 6 5

For Elyse and Sarah. L.W.G.
For Katie Morris, with many thanks. J.F.

The Saturday that Daddy moved away because of the divorce, he packed his blue car and a small trailer full. He sweated and puffed, but Mommy didn't help. And Katie was too sad to help.

When Daddy was finished, he knelt down next to Katie. He tried to explain things one more time. "Mommy and I can't live together anymore," he said. "We fight all the time, and we make each other unhappy. I don't want to leave you, but I have to." It was cold, and his words made white puffs. He circled Katie in his biggest hug. "I don't have a phone yet, but I'll call you Monday after work. I'll be here next Saturday to see you. I'll always be your Daddy."

Then he rolled out of the driveway in his blue car and was gone.

"Katie, come on in," Mommy called. She made hot chocolate and held Katie on her lap. For a while they rocked quietly.

That weekend, Katie was so sad she didn't want to do *anything*. She told her doll, Trisha, "You have to go away, too!" She threw Trisha into the wastebasket. Trisha was Katie's best doll, but that's how Katie felt.

She knew Mommy and Daddy quarreled a lot, but why did they have to get divorced? It seemed like somebody was throwing somebody else away.

All Monday, Katie's chest was like a heavy stone. When she woke up, she was happy for one second— until she remembered Daddy was gone. He didn't come in to say, "Rise and shine!" His chair at the breakfast table was empty. It seemed like there was a big hole in the air, next to the back door where Daddy's snow boots used to be.

While everybody else practiced subtracting in school, Katie studied the clouds. Her favorite lunch tasted awful. Walking home, she quarreled with her best friend.

When Daddy called from a pay phone that night, Katie felt even worse. She could hear traffic behind him, and he sounded as far off as the moon. After he hung up, Katie cried, and so did Mommy.

On Tuesday, Katie took Trisha to school. Trisha never left Katie all day.

Even with Trisha and the children near, Katie felt alone. And her thoughts were a jumble. One minute she tried to pretend Daddy was on a little trip. He hadn't really GONE AWAY. The next minute, she didn't care how far away he was. If he wanted to leave her, she'd just erase him, like a problem from the blackboard. The next minute, she worried that Daddy would be all alone at Christmas! Most of all, she was confused that Daddy and Mommy could stop loving each other. If that could happen, Daddy could forget her, too.

Mommy guessed how very terrible she felt when Katie wet the bed that night. Mommy changed the sheets and tucked her back in.

"You're sad, Katie. So am I. It's okay. We'll feel better someday."

But someday was a long way off.

On Wednesday, when Katie came home from school, there was a letter waiting for her! Mommy read it out loud. It said, "Dear Katie: Here is a very important phone number. It's mine! Now you can call whenever you want. Love, Daddy."

Katie dialed the number FAST, and Daddy answered on the first ring. "I hoped you'd call right away," he said.

Daddy told Katie what he was doing. Just now he was moving the sofa. For the third time. "It looks funny, Katie," he said. "You have to come Saturday and help me figure out where to put this stuff. You like moving furniture!"

Katie laughed. It was true. She moved the furniture in her dollhouse all the time.

"Isn't Mommy going to help you?"

"No," said Daddy. "She won't be my helper anymore because we won't be married. But you can. I'm not getting divorced from you, Katie."

Katie felt tears sting her eyes. "But you did go away, Daddy."

"I know," Daddy said. "But I didn't want to leave *you*, ever. We can talk about it on Saturday. You'll come visit me and sleep over at my apartment all night!"

"Okay," Katie said.

"Will Daddy ever come back?" she asked Mommy that night. Mommy was reading her a story about some ducks who always came back.

"Not to live, Katie. But he loves you. And he'll never stop being your daddy."

Katie pulled the blankets tightly under her chin. The house was dark and quiet, and the moon shone brightly in her window. Daddy wasn't like the ducks, she thought. Even though he felt sorry, he *was* gone.

Thursday and Friday went by slowly.

"What time is Daddy coming tomorrow?" Katie asked Friday night. She and Mommy had packed and repacked her suitcase.

"About nine," Mommy said. "You'll have Saturday and Sunday to spend together."

"Will Daddy and I visit every week?"

"Maybe not every single week, but often," Mommy said. Mommy explained that Katie might visit at Daddy's for longer sometimes, too. "You'll just be visiting, though," she said, "because your home is with me."

Mommy had explained before that Daddy AND Mommy each had wanted Katie to live with them, but there was only one Katie. Daddy traveled a lot, and it would be harder for him to care for Katie.

"Why can't Daddy just come back?" Katie asked. "I'll always keep my room clean." Maybe if she could be perfect, there'd be no more quarrels.

Mommy stroked her hair. "You don't have to be extra good," she said. "A divorce is never a child's fault. Nothing you did or didn't do made Daddy go away. And you can't bring him back. Getting divorced was something Daddy and I thought about for a long time. We had to do it, and it's going to be for always. But think about Saturday now. One thing at a time!"

On Saturday, Katie got up before Mommy. She put on a striped sweater Daddy had bought her and her new blue sneakers. She took her toast and milk to the window so she could look out.

For a long time, she watched the quiet street. Daddy had promised, but would he come?

Finally, finally, she saw the blue hood sweep around the corner. Soon Daddy's car purred in the driveway by the maple tree.

Katie ran out so fast Daddy didn't even have time to open the door. "My Katie!" Daddy said as she climbed in.

Mommy brought Trisha, a ball, two books, and the bag she and Katie had packed. Daddy laughed. "Are you sure you didn't forget anything?" he asked Katie.

"See you tomorrow!" Mommy said.

At Daddy's apartment on Saturday, they moved the chairs four times, the sofa two more times, the lamps all over, the rug left, then right. At last Daddy and Katie had everything just perfect.

"I've got a special spot for you, too," Daddy said. He showed Katie a shelf in the cabinet. "These are your things. Nobody can go in here except you, and they're for you when you visit."

On the shelf were the biggest box of crayons Katie had ever seen, three coloring books, and three books to read. There were watercolors, colored paper, a yo-yo, glue, string, and a pair of scissors.

Daddy played Go Fish with Katie, just like at home. Then Katie sat next to him and colored some pictures while he watched part of a ball game.

Later they ordered a pizza. Daddy put a silly candle on the pizza, as if it were a birthday cake. "It's a celebration of your first visit," he said. "This place seems more like a home with you here, Peanut."

While they ate, they watched the sun go down until the big buildings turned all gray and purple. Then the lights winked on in hundreds of windows.

Katie was very quiet.

"What's up?" Daddy asked.

"I was scared," Katie said. She didn't say all of what she was thinking, but Daddy guessed.

"Did you think I wouldn't come?"

"Mary never sees her daddy."

Daddy dropped his fork and took her hand. "I'm not Mary's daddy. I'm your daddy! And I'm right here, aren't I? Let's see." He patted his chest and pounded his forehead.

Katie giggled. Daddy was there.

"Even though I can't be with you every day anymore, I love you. I'll never fool you, Katie. When I say I'll see you, that means I'll be there."

"But maybe you'll forget me after a while."

"Never, ever, Katie. When you're worried, don't pay attention to any of those other daddies or what anybody else says. Ask me."

After that, Katie almost always visited Daddy on Saturdays. Often he'd take her to a movie or on a picnic or to the swimming pool. Daddy was getting to be a good cook, and Katie helped. Together they learned to make spaghetti sauce, baked potatoes, milkshakes, omelettès, and french toast.

The more she visited Daddy, the more his house did seem like a home. Daddy taped her pictures on his refrigerator. When Katie stayed all night, she slept on Daddy's sofa bed, which was in the perfect place in the living room. Sometimes her visits were even a little boring, just like being with Daddy on a regular old day at home.

Katie still felt hurt about the divorce, and she probably always would. It was hard each week when she and Daddy had to say good-bye. But in the world, there were things she could count on.

Home with Mommy was still home. And Mommy was feeling better, too. They could share a lot, like always. When Mommy joined a new exercise class, she showed Katie fancy steps and stretches.

Katie could call Daddy. He helped her learn his phone number by heart. Even if he wasn't home sometimes, or if either of them had to miss a Saturday, they could speak to each other.

When she was with Daddy, he had time for her. At home, in the old days, sometimes Mommy and Daddy were arguing, or Daddy was working when Katie wanted him to listen.

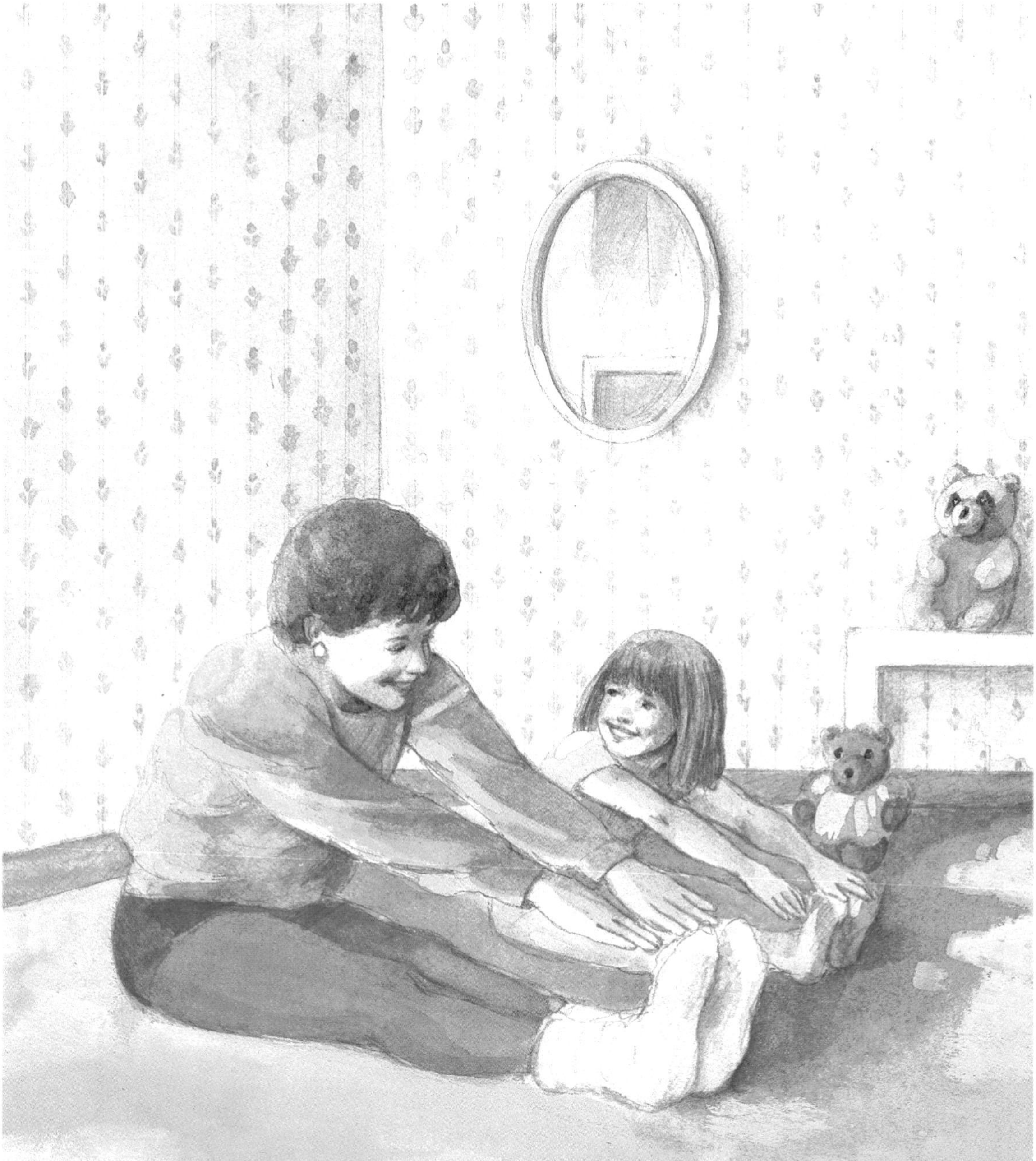

[redacted]

What happened to Mommy and Daddy was sad. But Katie's daddy didn't disappear, poof, when the divorce happened. When his blue car pulled into the driveway, bringing her home, he always said the same old thing.

"I'll be seeing you," Daddy said.

And Katie knew he would.